Once upon a time...

The birds flew in the sunny skies over a plateau tucked into

the side of a very tall mountain.

On that very plateau were trees, all sorts of plants, and an

exceptionally large egg!

The egg was green, yellow, blue, red, and all the shades between.

One day, the egg began to shake.

The egg began to bounce.

The egg rolled back and forth.

All sorts of scratchy and crackling sounds came from the egg.

A big crack zigged, then zagged until it went completely around the egg.

Out popped a tail!

Out popped a nose!

There it was, a broken egg!

There he was, a newly hatched dragon!

A dragon that was green, yellow, blue, red, and all the shades between!

There was a young boy named Remington,

and he could see the mountain from his home.

He always looked up and wondered what the plateau on the side of the

mountain was like. It was hard to imagine,

as there was always a smokey-like cloud around it.

Sometimes Remington wanted to be outside by himself.

Remington's little brother was very busy and messy!

Now, Mama and Papa told him that a

new little sister would be joining the family!

Remington thought that will be fun, but,

the plateau was fascinating to him.

"Some day, I will climb that plateau,

I will see what is up there!"

What Remington did not know, he was the

only one who could see the smokey plateau!

The day had come.

Remington packed extra lunch and water in his back pack.

He put on his best hiking shoes,

and of course he wore his explorer's hat!

Remington climbed the rocky side of the mountain.

It was fun and exciting!

"Wow!" Remington called out, "I'm climbing in the clouds!"

As the top was in sight, Remington could see

a big branch hanging over the edge.

"Just what I need to pull myself up on the plateau."

Remington said to himself as he grabbed on to it...

"YEOW!" Remington exclaimed as the branch lifted him in the air. The branch wasn't a branch at all! Remington was holding on to a dragon's tail!

Around came a tail with Remington attached!

There Remington was, shaking with fear as he looked into the
face of a mighty dragon!

"Now, just what are you?" asked the dragon.

"I'mmm a bbbboy, stuttered Remington.

"Oh, yes, the birds told me about boys. I believe I like boys."

The dragon was looking intently at Remington.

"Nnnnnott to eeeat, I hope!" squeaked Remington.

The dragon laughed as he put Remington down.

"Do you have a name, young boy?"

Out came a very shaky, "RRREMMMMiNNNNGTON."

"Well, Remington, my friends, the birds, named me Drake,
and I do NOT eat boys! In fact you are
the first boy I have ever seen!"

"The birds plant all kinds of things here.

I eat all sorts of plants.

I LOVE to eat onions!

They are my FAVORITE!"

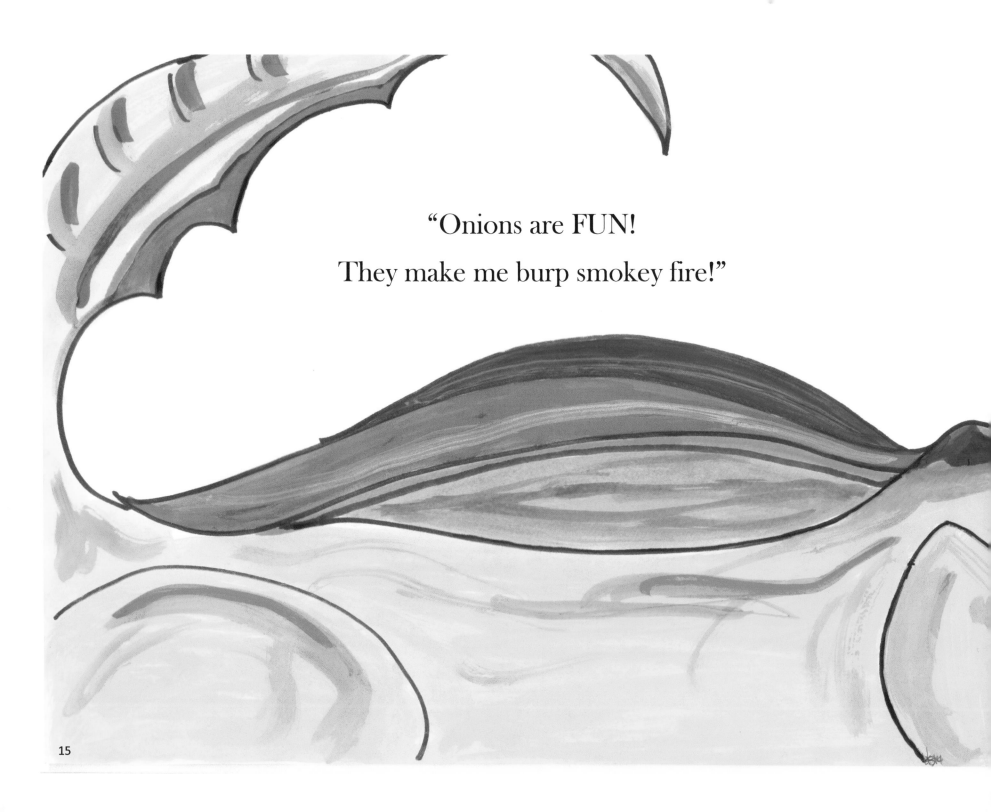

"Onions are FUN!

They make me burp smokey fire!"

Remington and Drake talked and asked each other questions.

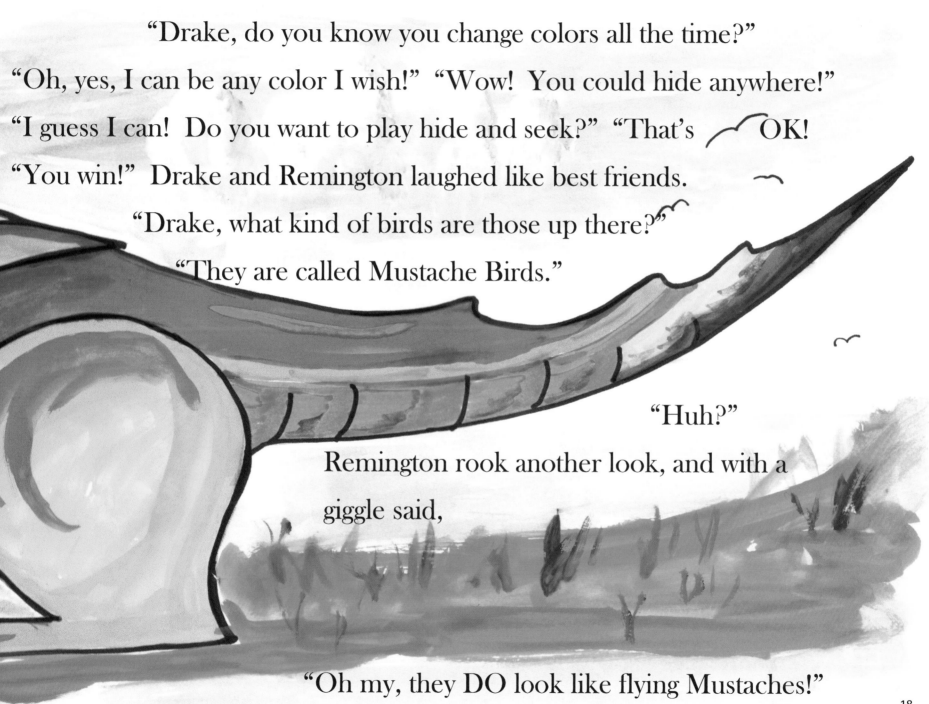

"Drake, do you know you change colors all the time?"

"Oh, yes, I can be any color I wish!" "Wow! You could hide anywhere!"

"I guess I can! Do you want to play hide and seek?" "That's   OK!

"You win!" Drake and Remington laughed like best friends.

"Drake, what kind of birds are those up there?"

"They are called Mustache Birds."

"Huh?"

Remington rook another look, and with a

giggle said,

"Oh my, they DO look like flying Mustaches!"

"Do you ever go down the mountain?" Remington asked.

"Oh, NO! How would I get down there? I might fall!

That's a long way down! That's too scary for me!"

Drake shook his head as he talked.

"NO, NO, NO, NO, NOOOOO!"

Remington looked at Drake and asked,

"Why don't you fly down? All dragons can fly!"

"What are you talking about?" asked Drake.

"Well, those big things on your back are folded up wings! You can open those wings, then flap them up and down like the birds do, the run really fast and jump up. You will fly just like the birds can."

Remington thought he explained that clearly.

"REALLY?"

Drake wasn't sure if he believed this.

"OK Remington, I will try!"

Drake was very excited at the thought of flying.

Drake did as Remington said.

He opened his wings wide and flapped them up and down.

Flapping away, Drake ran as fast as he could and jumped up.

"Look, Remington, look, I'm doing it, I'm flying!"

Drake was so excited that he FORGOT to flap his wings
up and down!

Drake crashed down in a cloud of dust!

"Are you all right?"

Remington was yelling as he ran towards Drake.

"I guess I can't forget to flap my wings
up AND down!" puffed Drake.

Drake didn't give up.

He flew around the mountain as Remington watched.

Drake was flying as though he had been doing it forever.

There he was, flying with his friends, the Mustache Birds.

Drake came back to Remington.

He was the happiest dragon ever!

"Thank you Remington! Flying is so fun!

I can see everywhere!"

"This has been the best day EVER!"
Remington exclaimed.

"I have climbed to the top of the plateau,
I have met a real live dragon, and
I have a new friend!"

With a GIGANTIC dragon smile,
Drake said,
"It has been the best day EVER for me too!"

"It's time for me to go home Drake. My Mama and Papa and my little brother will worry if I am late for dinner."

Remington was kind of worried that it was a long way back home.

"Remington, climb onto my back. I will FLY you home. We will get there quickly." said Drake.

"Yea!" Remington exclaimed. "Let's go!"

Drake the Dragon and Remington flew off the plateau and down the mountain. Remington held onto Drake tightly.

As they flew, Drake's colors changed to match the sky.

In a very short time they landed in the playground behind Remington's home.

"Thank you Drake! You are such a cool friend!

Wow, now your colors match the playground!

People can't even see you unless they look really, really hard!"

Drake did not tell Remington that he was the only person who could see him. Just like Remington was the only person who could see the plateau!

This was a secret for another time.

Drake smiled as he plucked a scale from his back and a hair from beside his ear.

Drake made a pendant using his hair as a chain and his color changing scale as a medallion.

"Wear this around your neck,
I will always know where you are
If you need me, hold the
medallion in your hand and
count to ten,
I will come as fast as I can fly!

Now, run home to dinner
and your family.
Thank you again for
THE BEST DAY EVER!"

As Drake flew away, Remington waved goodbye, and said to himself,
"I will see my new friend again soon!"

Later
my
friend ...

CPSIA information can be obtained at www.ICGtesting.com
Printed in the USA
BVIW120608280519
548936BV00001B/1